I'll Be the Water

A Story of a Grandparent's Love

Alec Aspinwall

Illustrated by Nicole Wong

TILBURY HOUSE PUBLISHERS, THOMASTON, MAINE

I never thought Grandpa was old. He wasn't just my grandfather. He was one of my best friends. We liked the same things, like peanut butter-and-banana sandwiches, digging in the dirt, and going fishing on hot summer days.

Sometimes we'd pretend his old car was a submarine and look for pirates or sunken treasure. It didn't matter where we went, because every place became an adventure with Grandpa.

Grandpa knew a lot about everything. I couldn't be with him for long without learning something. He would start a math lesson with a pocketful of change or turn over a rock and teach me about science.

Most of all, Grandpa and I loved to go fishing. We didn't care if we caught anything. Grandpa made me the captain of our boat. He made me feel like I could do anything I set my mind to.

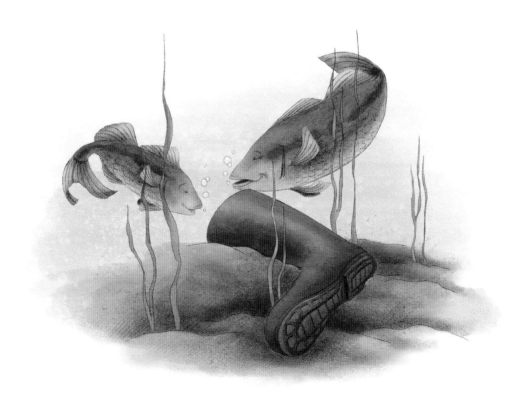

One day I noticed that Grandpa really was old. I saw his wrinkles for the first time, like his skin had grown too big for his face. Then I saw that Grandpa's hands shook when he put a worm on my fishhook, and he got up a little slower after we'd been digging in the garden.

"Grandpa, are you getting old?" I asked.

"Joshua," he said, "I've been getting old since I was a baby. I'm just gettin' better at it, that's all."

We laughed and offered a toast with our ice cream cones.

Then Grandpa went into the hospital. He said it was just for tests, but I felt scared.

"Grandpa," I said, "I wish you weren't so good at getting old."

He smiled and said, "I always have been an overachiever."

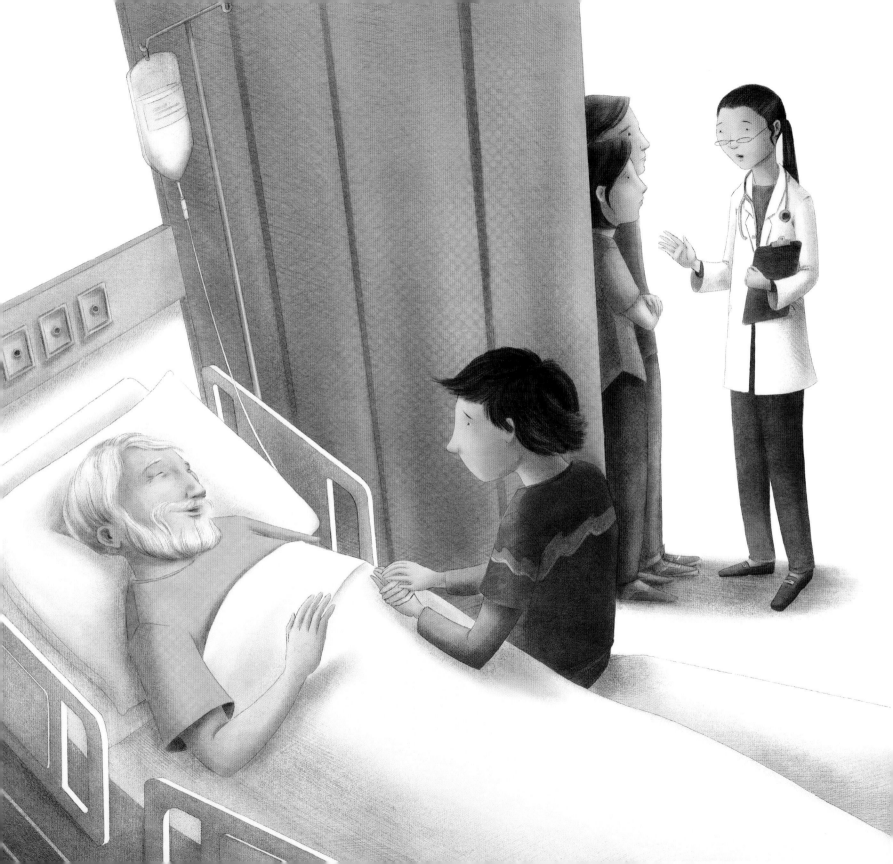

I asked my parents, "What if Grandpa doesn't get better? What if the doctors can't stop him from getting old?"

My dad said, "Don't worry, Joshua. Everything will be fine."

But Dad had said the same thing when my best friend Kenny moved away and when my dog Barker died, and those things were definitely not fine.

Grandpa finally got out of the hospital, and soon we were
back at the lake. He could tell by how quiet I was that
something was wrong, though.

"Joshua, you're biting even less than the fish," he said as
we ate our lunch. "What's on your mind? Are you trying
to find a way to make broccoli taste like chocolate?"

I never could keep a secret from him, so I asked, "Are you afraid of dying, Grandpa?"

Grandpa laughed and said, "You know, Joshua, nobody really knows what dying is like because nobody ever lives to tell about it. But I'm not afraid of dying. I still feel close to loved ones who have passed on before me, like your grandma. I don't think of her as being gone, because each memory of her is like a special gift I can unwrap again and again. And that's a gift I want to give you, too."

"You know," he said, "I was about your age when my daddy died in a train accident. I remember crying enough tears to fill two oceans and a bathtub. He had promised us kids that he would always be there for us. I thought he had broken his promise when he died."

It seemed like all the frogs and birds on the lake grew quiet to listen to Grandpa.

"But it turned out that he kept his promise after all. I just had to learn
to look for him with my heart instead of my eyes."

"Think of it this way," he said. "Today, you and I are
like two fish swimming together in this lake. When I die,
things will be different. I won't be a fish anymore,
but I'll become something even better.
I'll be the water.

"You might think I'm not with you, but we'll be closer than ever because you'll be surrounded by my love. I'll be wherever you go and by your side in whatever you do."

I thought about the fish and the water beneath our boat, and about Grandpa and me, and then I began to understand.

"Will you be there if I get into trouble at school?" I asked.

"I'll be there," he said.

"What if I have to go on stage in front of everyone and play the piano?"

"I'll be in the front row."

"Can you help me on my math tests?"

Grandpa laughed. "I've never been much for math, Joshua, but we'll give it a go."

We laughed a lot that afternoon, and even though we didn't catch a thing, it was the best fishing trip we ever had.

It was also our last fishing trip. Grandpa went back into the hospital soon after, and the doctors weren't able to fix him. When my parents told me that Grandpa had died, I cried enough to fill three oceans and two bathtubs.

I hurt inside for a long time. But then I began to see with my heart instead of my eyes, and I didn't feel so alone. As I grew older, I could see that Grandpa had kept his promise. His last gift to me was one that would always be there.

Now when my daughter and I go fishing or toast with ice cream cones or dig in the dirt or go on imaginary adventures, I teach her what Grandpa taught me.

She knows we never have to feel alone or afraid, because we are surrounded by a love that lasts forever.

For all who have been our past mentors
and remain our ever-present guides.
—A.A.

Text © 2020 by Alec Aspinwall • Illustrations © 2020 by Nicole Wong
Hardcover ISBN 978-0-88448-776-0
Tilbury House Publishers • 12 Starr Street
Thomaston, Maine 04861 • www.tilburyhouse.com

Library of Congress Control Number: 2020935128
Designed by Frame25 Productions • Printed in Korea
15 16 17 18 19 20 XXX 10 9 8 7 6 5 4 3 2 1